For Jason

First published in the United States of America in July 2014
by Walker Books for Young Readers, an imprint of Bloomsbury Publishing, Inc.
www.bloomsbury.com
Bloomsbury is a registered trademark of Bloomsbury Publishing Plc

For information about permission to reproduce selections from this book, write to
Permissions, Walker BFYR, 1385 Broadway, New York, New York 10018
Bloomsbury books may be purchased for business or promotional use. For information on bulk purchases please contact Macmillan Corporate and Premium Sales Department at specialmarkets@macmillan.com

Library of Congress Cataloging-in-Publication Data
Yoon, Salina.
Penguin and pumpkin / Salina Yoon.
pages cm
Summary: Curious about what fall is like in places that are not always white, Penguin and his friends go to a pumpkin farm and bring back a surprise for Penguin's brother, Pumpkin, who couldn't come with them.
ISBN 978-0-8027-3732-8 (hardcover) • ISBN 978-0-8027-3733-5 (reinforced)
ISBN 978-0-8027-3769-4 (e-book) • ISBN 978-0-8027-3770-0 (e-PDF)
[1. Autumn—Fiction. 2. Penguins—Fiction. 3. Pumpkins—Fiction. 4. Brothers—Fiction.] I. Title.
PZ7.Y817Pfd 2014 [E]—dc23 2013039745

Art created digitally using Adobe Photoshop
Typeset in Maiandra
Book design by Nicole Gastonguay

Printed in China by Leo Paper Products, Heshan, Guangdong
1 3 5 7 9 10 8 6 4 2 (hardcover)
1 3 5 7 9 10 8 6 4 2 (reinforced)

All papers used by Bloomsbury Publishing, Inc., are natural, recyclable products made from wood grown in well-managed forests. The manufacturing processes conform to the environmental regulations of the country of origin.

Penguin and Pumpkin

Salina Yoon

WALKER BOOKS FOR YOUNG READERS
AN IMPRINT OF BLOOMSBURY
NEW YORK LONDON NEW DELHI SYDNEY

It was fall, and very white on the ice, as always—which made Penguin curious.

I wonder what fall looks like off the ice.

Let's go to the farm and find out!

Penguin's baby brother,
Pumpkin, waddled over.

"I'm sorry, Pumpkin. But it's too far for a fledgling."

Grandpa agreed. “Maybe next year, Pumpkin.”

Penguin, Bootsy, and their friends headed to the farm.

The journey was long, as Penguin . . .

. . . looked,

. . . and looked,

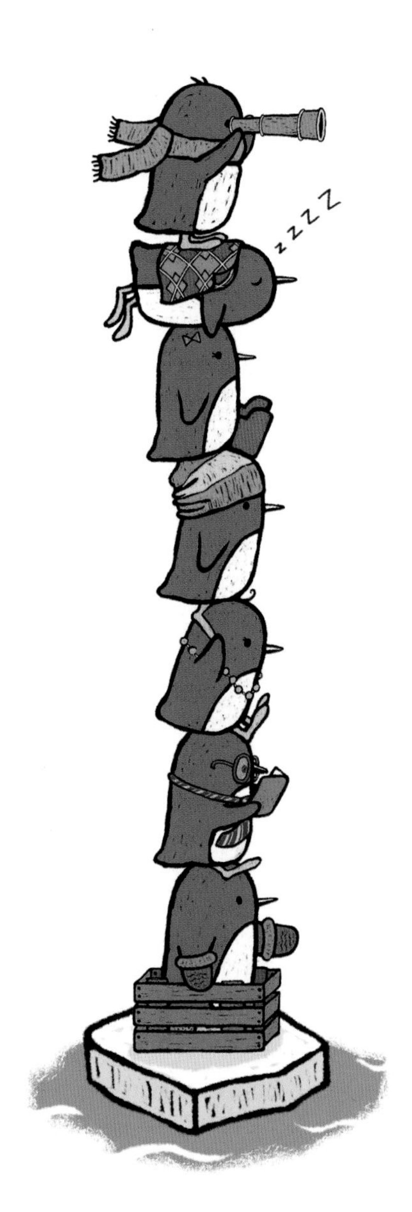

. . . and looked for signs of land.

Finally, the penguins arrived.

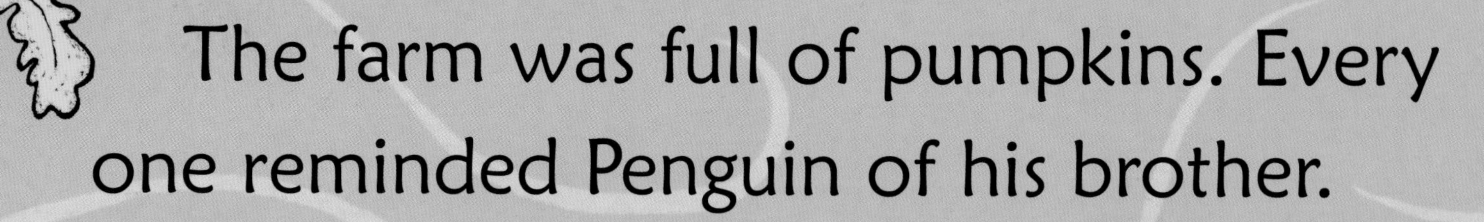

The farm was full of pumpkins. Every one reminded Penguin of his brother.

Then Penguin looked up.

The penguins each picked out a pumpkin.

Some were smooth.

Some were bumpy.

Some were long.

Some were curved.

Every pumpkin was loved.

Penguin had a different idea.

They rode back home with
their fall harvest.

Are we there yet?
z z z Z

The fall explorers were excited to share their treasures from the farm.

But where was Pumpkin?

Penguin found a clue.

"What are you doing over here?"

"Since you wouldn't let us come, we decided to have our own fall adventure."

“We imagined . . .

. . . fall on the harvest moon,

. . . fall on spooky Saturn,

. . . and even fall on the Red Planet!”

“You have a space-tacular imagination,” said Penguin.

"But I wish I got to see
what fall REALLY looks like."
Pumpkin sighed.

“See fall?” thought Penguin.

"Wait right here, Pumpkin!"

Penguin took the crate up on a cliff.

Grandpa and Bootsy followed a trail of leaves that led them right to Pumpkin.

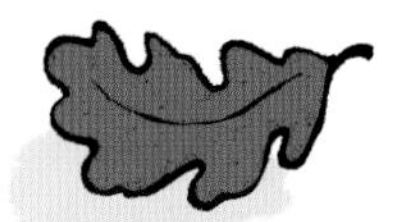

"A pumpkin for Pumpkin! A perfect match!"

Penguin finally returned. “What does fall really look like?” asked Pumpkin eagerly.

“Look up!” said Grandpa.

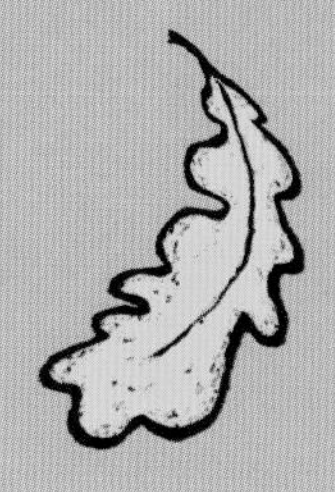

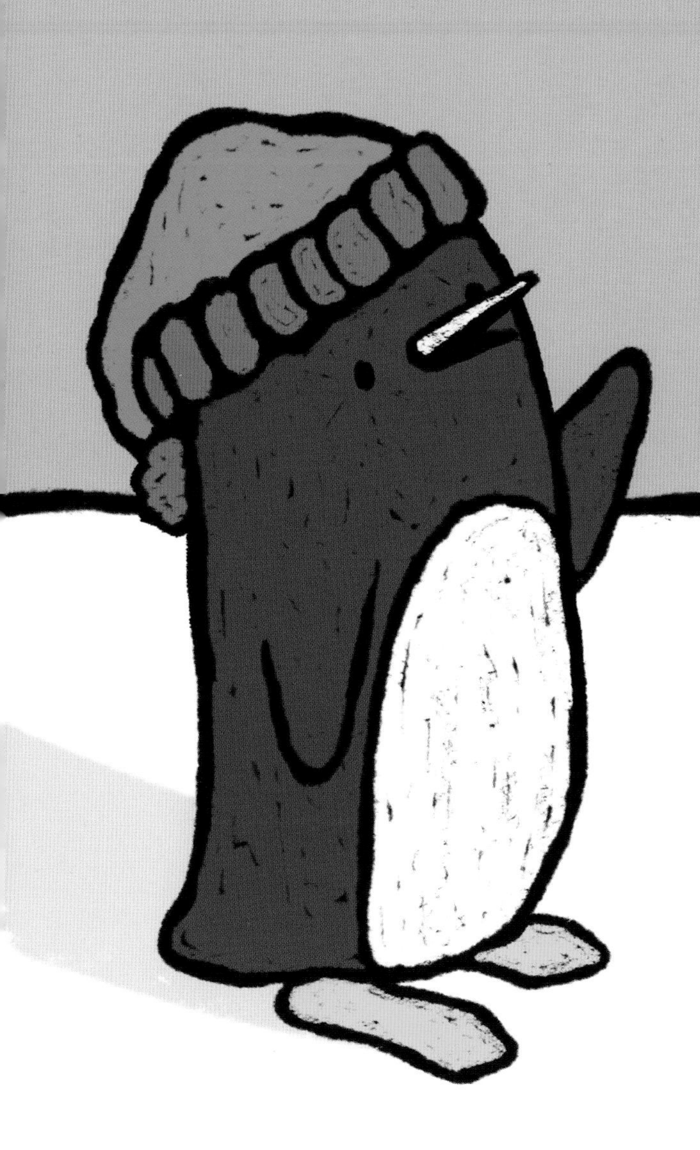

“Fall looks like . . .”

". . . snowing leaves!"